leapfrog

Rhyme Time

What a Frog!

First published in 2007 by
Franklin Watts
338 Euston Road
London
NW1 3BH

Franklin Watts Australia
Level 17/207 Kent Street
Sydney
NSW 2000

Text © Sue Graves 2007
Illustration © Claire Barker 2007

A CIP catalogue record for this book is available
from the British Library.

ISBN 978 0 7496 7102 0 (hbk)
ISBN 978 0 7496 7794 7 (pbk)

Series Editor: Jackie Hamley
Editor: Melanie Palmer
Series Advisor: Dr Barrie Wade
Series Designer: Peter Scoulding

Printed in China

Franklin Watts is a division of
Hachette Children's Books,
an Hachette Livre UK company.

What a Frog!

by Sue Graves

Illustrated by Claire Barker

W
FRANKLIN WATTS
LONDON • SYDNEY

It was sports day
at the frog pond.
All the frogs were there.

The judges sat along
the bank on big, brown,
wooden chairs.

7

First there was the
swimming race.

Alfie swam quite fast.

9

But George and Freddy
beat him,

and Alfie came in last.

Next there was the
leaping game.
Alfie did his very best.

But he tripped and missed
the lily pad ...

14

and landed on his chest.

17

The diving test was last
of all.

Alfie took a running jump.

1st	Freddy
2nd	George
last	Alfie

But he slipped ...

and flipped,

then spun around ...

and landed with a thump!

23

Then the judges started
clapping.

The fathers stamped
their feet.

The mothers got excited
and stood up on their seats.

"What a frog!"
the judges shouted.

"What a frog to dive like that!"

"Our Alfie is a winner.
He's a real acrobat!"

31

Leapfrog has been specially designed to fit the requirements of the National Literacy Strategy. It offers real books for beginning readers by top authors and illustrators. There are 67 Leapfrog stories to choose from:

* hardback